Mother, May I?

written by **Lynn Plourde** illustrated by **Amy Wummer**

Dutton Children's Books ★ New York

To Danica, with love from your brother, Aunt Lynn
L.P.

To my mother, Alice
A.W.

CIP Data is available.

Published in the United States by Dutton Children's Books,
a division of Penguin Young Readers Group
345 Hudson Street, New York, New York 10014
www.penguin.com

Designed by Beth Herzog

Manufactured in China
First Edition
ISBN 0-525-46988-5

1 3 5 7 9 10 8 6 4 2

Mother, may I, on your special day,

be the mom to **_you_** today?

Now you be a good girl,

and I'll bring you a big surprise. . . .

Open wide!

May I fix your hair
extra fancy?

Sit still.

How 'bout I help
with your makeup?

Smile!

Mother, may I
clean the house?

Just the way you like it.

Or maybe I'll take you shopping.

How 'bout one of each, Mom?

I could make your headache all better . . .

then tuck you in tight for a nap.

Sweet dreams.

Mother, may I
        help you catch up on your work?

All done!

Looks like you could use a bath.

Here's Duckie.

Oops—maybe I need more practice being a mom.

'Cept there's one mom thing
I know how to do just right.

MOTHER, MAY I . . .

say **"I LOVE YOU!"**